GO, MO, GO!
DINOSAUR DASH

HODDER CHILDREN'S BOOKS

First published in Great Britain in 2017 by Hodder and Stoughton

1 3 5 7 9 10 8 6 4 2

A CIP catalogue record for this book
is available from the British Library.

ISBN 978 1 444 93401 4

Printed and bound in Great Britain by
Clays Ltd, St Ives plc

The paper and board used in this book
are made from wood from responsible sources.

Hodder Children's Books
An imprint of
Hachette Children's Group
Part of Hodder and Stoughton
Carmelite House
50 Victoria Embankment
London EC4Y 0DZ

An Hachette UK Company
www.hachette.co.uk

www.hachettechildrens.co.uk

GO, MO, GO!
DINOSAUR DASH

Mo Farah

Hodder Children's Books

It was a beautiful bright Sunday morning and little Mo and his friends had just been for a run in the park.

"Where shall we go next?" smiled Vern, jogging up and down on the spot to keep his legs full of running.

"Let's run to the North Pole!" said Lily. **"We can have a race with some polar bears!"**

1

"Let's run to China," said Banjo. "We can go jogging with some pandas!"

"Let's run to the moon!" said Lyra. "We can play hide and seek in the craters!"

Little Mo retied his shoelaces, stroked his chin and then **smiled**.

"I know!" he said. "Let's run **somewhere we've *never* run before!**"

"Where?" asked Vern.

"Backwards!" said Mo.

"BACKWARDS?" frowned Lyra.

"Yes, backwards!" nodded Mo.

Lily looked over her shoulder. "But no

one runs backwards," she frowned.

"All the more reason to do it!" said Mo.

"But what if we fall over?" asked Vern.

"If we fall over, we'll just have to pick ourselves up!" laughed Mo.

"What if we bump into something?" asked Banjo.

"If we find the **BIGGEST**, widest open space to run backwards in, we can make sure there is nothing to bump into!" said Mo.

Lily smiled at Vern, Vern smiled at Banjo, Banjo smiled at Lyra and then everyone smiled at Mo.

"Backwards does sound rather fun," they nodded.

"We could hold hands while we're running!" smiled Banjo.

"Good idea," said Lily. "If we hold hands we can stick together!"

"And we can keep up with each other," smiled Lyra.

"And fall over together!" chuckled Vern.

"Then let's do it!" cheered Mo.

The biggest open space in the park was very big, very open and very spacy indeed.

"On your marks!" said Banjo, glancing at Lily and taking one last look over his shoulder.

"Get set!" said Lyra, offering her free hand to Vern.

"OG!" yelled Mo.

5

Slow to start, quick to rally, the five runners were soon hurtling backwards across the park like a **super-duper express human paper chain** (in reverse).

"Let's go faster!" said Vern, raising Lyra's arm high into the air.

"Let's go faster than fast!" said Banjo, squeezing Lily and Mo's hands tight.

"Let's go faster than faster than fast AND close our eyes too!" laughed Vern, raising both arms, closing both eyes, tripping over both feet and sending all five friends **crashing to the floor.**

"Let's not," groaned Mo, yanking his

trainers from a tangle of legs and giving
the back of his head a rub.

"Sorry," said Vern, opening his eyes and
rubbing his shoulder. "That wasn't meant
to happen."

"No it wasn't," groaned Banjo. "We were
meant to stay on our feet."

"Where are my feet?" asked Lyra, tugging at her knees.

"Never mind your feet, where is the park??" gulped Lily.

The five friends looked round and rubbed their eyes.

"Where are the flower beds?" frowned Vern, turning his head in all directions.

"Where are the swings? asked Lyra.

"Where are the squirrels?" asked Banjo.

"Where's the duck pond?" asked Lily.

"RUN!" shouted

Mo.

Quick as a lizard-lick Mo sprang to his feet and started sprinting forwards towards the nearest valley.

Lily, Lyra, Banjo and Vern **jumped** to their feet and sped after him.

"Why are we running?" gasped Banjo.

"DINOSAURS ARE COMING!" shouted Mo.

"DINOSAURS!?" gasped Banjo.

"YES, DINOSAURS!!!!!" yelled Mo.

Lily peered over her shoulder. Mo was right, a **HUGE herd of dinosaurs were stomping straight towards them!**

"I thought dinosaurs were **extinct!**"
gasped Lily.

"Not in prehistoric times!" shouted Mo.
"We've run backwards so fast we must
have run back in time!"

"RUN BACK IN TIME???!"
gasped Lily.

"All the way back to prehistoric times,"
frowned Mo.

"But that means . . . that means . . ."

Lily wasn't sure what it meant.

"It means dinosaurs are **very
much ALIVE!**" yelled Mo.
"And if they catch us, **WE'LL be
the ones who are extinct!**"

Mo and his four friends raced across

the dusty plain in the direction of a prehistoric valley.

"If we can reach the valley before the dinosaurs catch us we can find somewhere to hide!" shouted Mo.

"TREES!" pointed Vern. "We can hide up one of those trees!"

The prehistoric trees that lined the valley were **HUGE**, they had trunks as wide as roundabouts and leaves as big as picnic blankets. As soon as the five friends reached one they climbed straight up the trunk and **right to the very top branch.**

"Find a leaf and roll yourself up inside it!" said Mo. "The dinosaurs will never know we're here!"

Vern, Lily, Banjo and Lyra did exactly as Mo had told them.

"It's like being rolled up inside a carpet!" whispered Lily.

"I feel like a **great big green sausage roll!**" whispered Vern.

"Don't make a sound," whispered Mo, peering out of his leafy hiding place. **"Don't make a move!"**

The ground was shaking. The dinosaurs were approaching.

The closer they came, the bigger they looked. Their tails were as long as ski runs,

their bodies were as round as petrol tankers, their necks were as **tall as building cranes** and when they lifted their heads their eyes came as high as the tree tops!

Mo kept very still as one by one the dinosaurs inspected the leaves.

"They're sniffing!" whispered Mo.

"Sniffing for us I bet!" whispered Vern.

"They're looking for lunch," whispered Mo.

"I don't want to be a dinosaur's lunch!" whispered Banjo.

"Or breakfast," whispered Lily.

"Or tea," whispered Lyra.

"Quiet," whispered Mo.

The five friends held their breath and stayed as still as a stuck stamp.

"We're in luck!" gasped Mo. "They're herbivores!"

"What are herbivores?" asked Lyra.

"Dinosaurs that **only** eat greens!" whispered Vern.

"PHEW!!" sighed Banjo.

"RUN!"
shouted Mo.

Suddenly Mo uncurled himself from his leafy hiding place and sprinted back along the top branch.

"Why are we running?" asked Lyra.

"Because wrapping ourselves up in leaves makes us **look like leaves!**" shouted Mo. "We don't want to get eaten by mistake!"

"I don't want to get eaten by anything!" puffed Lily.

Mo, Lyra, Lily, Banjo and Vern climbed down the trunk of the prehistoric tree and sped along the valley floor.

"Are they chasing us?" gasped Lily, clearing a path with her arms. The grass was shoulder height, the moss came up to her knees!

"I don't think so," shouted Mo. "It takes more than a few leaves to fill the tummy of a brontosaurus!"

"They're still eating their lunch!" shouted Banjo. "I just heard one of them do a burp!"

"That wasn't a burp," said Lyra, pinching her nose.

Deeper and deeper into the valley they raced.

"Duck behind that big rock!" pointed Mo. "We can get our breath back there!"

The four friends joined Little Mo behind a craggy grey boulder and slid their bottoms to the floor.

"That was close!" panted Mo.

"Did you see the **size of their teeth?!**" gasped Banjo.

"Did you see the size of their tongues?!" panted Vern.

"Did you see the length of their necks?!" puffed Lily.

"Imagine being swallowed by a brontosaurus!" said Lyra.

"It would be like going **down a flume at a water park!**" smiled Banjo.

"Only not half as much fun," frowned Vern.

"Especially when you came out the other end," grimaced Banjo.

"The important thing is we're safe," said Mo.

"RUN!"

Lily, Lyra, Banjo and Vern jumped to their feet.

"Why are we running now?" gasped Vern, following hot on Mo's heels.

"T REXES!"

shouted Mo.

"T REXES!!!!!!" gasped Lyra.

"T Rexes don't eat greens, they eat . . ."

"CHILDREN!!!!" shouted Lily.

Banjo glanced back in the direction
of their hiding place. It wasn't a craggy
grey boulder any more, it was a craggy
grey boulder turned to dust! A T Rex
had flattened it with one stamp of its
gigantic foot!!

24

"They look **really hungry!!!**" squeaked Vern, sprinting for all he was worth.

"Follow me!" shouted Mo, cutting away from the valley floor and **weaving his way through a maze tree trunks**, bushes and undergrowth.

"Conkersaurus shells!" he pointed. "Look over there on the forest floor! We can hide inside those giant conker shells!"

Mo sprinted hard and then **dived inside one of the giant green conker shells** that was littering the forest floor.

"They're as big as a Mini!!!" panted Lily, crawling inside a shell of her own.
"Move over!" panted Vern, squeezing inside an extra big one with Lyra and Banjo.

"Quiet!" warned Mo. **"The T Rexes are coming!"**

Vern, Lily, Banjo and Lyra peered nervously out of their hiding places and then braced themselves as the ground began to shake.

Mo pressed his fingers to his lips
and then stiffened as the stampede of
**hungry T Rexes went
thundering by.**

"We've lost them!" he cheered, giving his friends the **double thumbs up** and then crawling out of his hiding place.

"Thank goodness," gasped Lily. "We're safe."

"RUN!" shouted Mo.

Lily, Lyra, Banjo and Vern sprang to their feet and raced hot on the heels of Mo.

"Why are we running again?!" panted Banjo.

"GIGANTOSAURUSES!!"

shouted Mo.

"Heading this way!!!!"

"They sound big!" gasped Vern.

"They're **bigger**

than

BIG!"

shouted Mo. "They're ginormous!"

"What do gigantosauruses eat?" puffed Lyra.

"T REXES!" shouted Mo. "And children if they fancy a starter! We need to get out of the valley, it's **far too dangerous** to be running around here!"

"You lead, we'll follow!" panted Vern.

Mo led the way, sprinting full pelt up hills, through trees, across streams, round boulders, over fallen tree trunks, under giant toadstools, **on and on and on.**

"RUN!" he shouted as velociraptors bounded from bushes.

"RUN!" he shouted as sabre-toothed tigers rocketed from rocks.

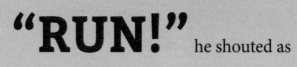

"RUN!" he shouted as

diplodocuses loomed from lakes.

And run they did; full pelt, **as fast as they could**, down slopes, through grasses, along fallen tree trunks,

across marshes, past giant dandelions and out of the valley and into the wide open desert at the far end.

"There are dinosaurs **everywhere!**" gasped Lily, dropping to her knees.

"No wonder," said Mo. "Look where we've just come from!"

"At least we've escaped the dinosaurs!" panted Mo. "All we need to do now is work out **how to get home!!**"

"Look, I can see an aeroplane," said
Vern, "up there in the sky! An aeroplane
has come to save us!"

"RUN!" shouted Mo.

Lily, Banjo, Lyra and Vern climbed wearily to their feet.

"Not again!" they gasped.

"It's not an aeroplane it's a **PTERODACTYL!**" shouted Mo.

"Do pterodactyls eat fatty balls or children?" asked Banjo, staring up at the sky.

"Fatty balls haven't been invented yet!" shouted Mo. "Does that answer your question!?"

"I can hear it **screeching!**" gasped Lily.

"I can hear it **flapping!**" gasped Banjo.

Banjo and Lily were right. The hungry pterodactyl had spotted the five children and **was homing in on its lunch.**

"Keep running!" shouted Mo. "If we can get to the other side of the desert we can find a new place to hide."

On and on they ran, faster and faster they sped.

"I can see its shadow!" gasped Lyra,

looking over her shoulder and finding the wings of the pterodactyl **looming overhead.**

"I can see its tonsils!" gasped Banjo, looking over his shoulder to find the beak of the pterodactyl **opening wide**.

"It's going to catch us!" gasped Lily.

"It's going to gobble us!" gasped Vern.

"It's turning around!" shouted Mo. **"Look it's flying away!"** he cheered.

Mo was right. With its wide open beak just centimetres from Lily's ponytail, the hungry pterodactyl had suddenly applied the brakes, wheeled around and **soared away into the distance.**

"Something must have frightened it!" gasped Lyra.

"I wonder what?" frowned Vern.

"That's what," pointed Mo.

"LOOK!"

Lyra, Vern, Lily and Banjo followed the direction of Mo's pointing finger.

There in front of them, towering above a field of golden corn, was a **giant prehistoric scarecrow!**

"Who do you think made it?" asked Lyra.

"Cavemen probably," said Mo.

"Cavemen definitely," said Lyra, **pointing over Mo's shoulder** in the direction of the cornfield.

Mo and the four friends turned towards the cornfield. A troop of hairy cavemen were **trudging towards them, brandishing heavy stone age clubs.**

"I didn't think cavemen were around in dinosaur times?" said Lyra.

"Maybe they ran back in time too," frowned Mo.

"I think they must have planted the cornfield," whispered Vern. "They probably turn the corn into stone age bread."

"And stone age rolls," whispered Lily.

"And stone age croissants," whispered Banjo.

"Stop," said Mo. "You're making me hungry. Now **remember to smile.** We want the cavemen to see that we are friendly."

Lily, Vern, Banjo and Lyra gathered beside Mo and waved as the cavemen drew nearer.

"We could ask them for a drink," said Lily.

"We could ask them how to get home," said Banjo.

"Good idea," said Mo.

"RUN!"

Suddenly Mo was sprinting again. Not in the direction of the cornfield but as far away from the cavemen as he could get.

"Why are we running again?" gasped Banjo, **hurtling hot on the heels** of Lyra, Lily and Vern. "I thought we were going to be their friends?"

"They've spotted our trainers!" shouted Mo. "Trainers haven't been invented yet. They want to **steal our trainers!!!**"

It was true. Clubs waving, chests thumping, the cavemen had only one thing on their minds.

"Why do they want to steal our trainers?" panted Lyra.

"So they can **run away from dinosaurs as fast as we can!**" shouted Mo.

With no time to waste and a gang of envious cavemen on their heels, the five friends **sprinted for all they were worth.**

"First we're running away from dinosaurs," gasped Banjo, "now we're running from cavemen!"

"It's a good job we're good at running!" said Lily.

"It would be an even better job if we could find our way home!" panted Vern.

"We need to run to the top of that mountain," pointed Mo. "If we run to the top of that mountain we might be able to see the way home!"

The mountain slope soared **high and steep.** Black as a caveman's scowl, slippery as a puddle of marbles, it was **no place for bare feet** and no place to carry the heavy weight of a stone age club.

"We're losing them!" shouted Lyra, looking back down the mountainside at the cavemen. "Their feet keep slipping on the stones!"

"Excellent!" cheered Mo. "Three cheers for training shoes," he whooped.

"I want to go home!" shouted Lily.

"Me too!" shouted Banjo, Lyra and Vern.

"So do the cavemen," shouted Mo. "See, they've given up the chase!"

Far below at the base of the mountain, the hairy, jealous, sweaty but shoeless cavemen were **racing back to their corn.** High up the mountainside, five pairs of dusty trainers were pounding.

"Keep running," shouted Mo. "If we can make it to the very top, I'm sure we will see the way home."

"I hope you're right," panted Banjo. "I miss my teddy."

"I miss my dog," panted Lily.

"I miss my cat," panted Lyra.

"I've got homework to do," gasped Vern.

"WE'RE THERE!" shouted Mo, **bounding like a gazelle** to the very tiptop of the slope and punching the air with his hands.

"RUN!"
he shouted.

"Run?" gasped Vern.

"Run?" panted Lyra

"Run?" squeaked Banjo.

"Why do you want us to run!!!!!?" puffed Lily. "We've **only just** got to the top of the mountain!"

Mo clapped his hands to his head and stared down at his feet in dismay.

"It's not a mountain, it's a **VOLCANO!**" he gulped. "There's a crater at the top of this volcano and it's about to **ERUPT!**"

"RUN BACKWARDS AGAIN," Mo hollered. **"THERE'S NO TIME FOR US TO TURN AROUND!"**

Vern, Banjo, Lily and Lyra began back-pedalling fast.

"I can't see where I'm going again!" shouted Lily.

"I'm losing my balance again," wobbled Vern.

"Hold hands!" shouted Mo. **"Run backwards, hold hands and stick together!!!"**

The slopes of the volcano were **shaking** now and the sides of the volcano were **cracking.** With an almighty rumble and a tumultuous belch, the crater at the top crumbled and then suddenly exploded like a humungous firework. Steam whistled into the atmosphere as **searing hot lava tumbled and treacled down the prehistoric slopes.**

"**LAVA!**" shouted Mo, sprinting backwards as fast as he could.

"**RED HOT LAVA!**" shouted Banjo, trying his best not to fall over.

"**RUN FOR YOUR LIVES!**" shouted Mo, as wave after wave of hot lava

surged from
the bubbling crater
and poured down the slopes
like strawberry custard towards the
children's retreating feet.

Vern, Banjo, Lily and Lyra gulped hard
and kept galloping backwards as fast as
their trainers would carry them.

"First we're running backwards for fun,
now we're running backwards for our
lives!" gasped Vern.

"Just keep running!" shouted Lily. "Talk less, **run more!**"

Bravely, boldly, blindly and backwards the five friends bowled down the slopes.

"The lava's getting closer!" panted Lily.

"My knees are getting hotter!" gasped Vern.

"My ankle socks are starting to smoke!" winced Lyra.

"My laces have come undone!" gasped Banjo, glancing down at his feet.

Mo looked over his shoulder at Banjo's laces. They were flapping round his legs like **cheese strings in a hurricane.**

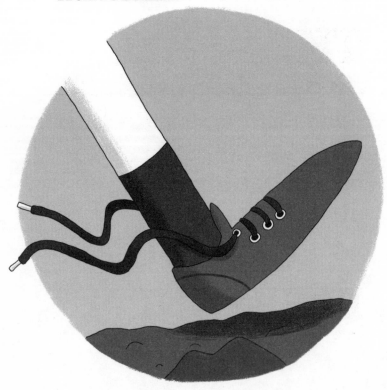

"MIND YOU DON'T TRIP OVER THEM!" he shouted.

But it was too late. With a jolt, a lurch and a clumsiest of trips, Banjo lassoed his own ankles and went **catapulting backwards through the air.**

"LOOK OUT, EVERYONE!"

he squealed, closing his eyes tightly and
bracing himself for every lump,
bump and bruise that was about to come
his way.

Eyes shut, hands clasped, **the five out of control runners cartwheeled backwards down the mountain.** Only at the very bottom of the volcano slope did they dare to open their eyes.

Mo was the first one to look in all directions. To his relief and his surprise they weren't **up to their necks in lava**, but daffodils!

"We're back in the park!" he gasped. "Look! No more dinosaurs, no more cavemen, no more red hot lava! We've tumbled backwards down the prehistoric mountain **so fast**, we've ended up all the way back where we began!!"

Lily, Vern, Lyra and Banjo rubbed their
eyes and clapped their hands.

"There's the swings!" pointed Lyra.

"There's the squirrels!" pointed Banjo.

"There's the duck pond!" pointed Vern.

"Where's the flower bed?" asked Lily.

"We're lying in it," gulped Mo.

"Ooh dear, I've squashed some lovely yellow flowers," said Lily.

"And I've squashed some very pretty red ones," said Lyra.

"I do hope the park keeper doesn't see us!" said Banjo. **"He won't be very happy with us at all."**

"RUN!" shouted Mo!

LOOK OUT
FOR MORE

GO, MO, GO!

ADVENTURES

"I bet the Rocky Mountains rock!"

Mo and his friends are excited for
a mountain adventure, until they find
out that the Rocky Mountains really do
rock – from *side* to *side* ...

But what is making the ground shake?

Watch out, here comes a
HUGE HAIRY FOOT ...

RUN!